PUFFIN

PRIMEVAL
A RIP
IN TIME

Books in the Primeval series

PRIMEVAL
A RIP IN TIME

Adapted by Kay Woodward

PUFFIN

PUFFIN BOOKS

Published by the Penguin Group
Penguin Books Ltd, 80 Strand, London WC2R ORL, England
Penguin Group (USA) Inc., 375 Hudson Street, New York, New York 10014, USA
Penguin Group (Canada), 90 Eglinton Avenue East, Suite 700, Toronto, Ontario, Canada M4P 2Y3
(a division of Pearson Penguin Canada Inc.)
Penguin Ireland, 25 St Stephen's Green, Dublin 2, Ireland (a division of Penguin Books Ltd)
Penguin Group (Australia), 250 Camberwell Road, Camberwell, Victoria 3124, Australia
(a division of Pearson Australia Group Pty Ltd)
Penguin Books India Pvt Ltd, 11 Community Centre, Panchsheel Park, New Delhi – 110 017, India
Penguin Group (NZ), 67 Apollo Drive, Rosedale, North Shore 0632, New Zealand
(a division of Pearson New Zealand Ltd)
Penguin Books (South Africa) (Pty) Ltd, 24 Sturdee Avenue, Rosebank,
Johannesburg 2196, South Africa

Penguin Books Ltd, Registered Offices: 80 Strand, London WC2R ORL, England

puffinbooks.com

First published 2008
I

Text copyright © Impossible Pictures, 2008
Photographs copyright © Impossible Pictures, 2008
Adapted by Kay Woodward
All rights reserved

Set in Times New Roman
Typeset by Palimpsest Book Production Limited, Grangemouth, Stirlingshire
Made and printed in England by Clays Ltd, St Ives plc

British Library Cataloguing in Publication Data
A CIP catalogue record for this book is available from the British Library

ISBN: 978-0-141-32391-6

A RIP IN TIME

It was night and the crowds of frantic shoppers had driven home hours ago. Now the out-of-town supermarket was virtually deserted, apart from a lone cleaner who mopped the floor, working his way up one aisle and down the next. Nodding to the rhythm of the music blaring through his headphones, it took a moment for him to notice a faint thumping in the background. When he looked up, he saw a woman hammering urgently at the glass doors. She had long dark hair and fine features.

The cleaner smiled at the stupidity of the general public. The shop had been closed for hours, so she'd just have to make her purchases tomorrow. Then, without removing his headphones, he carried on making neat, glossy arcs with his wet mop.

Outside the supermarket, the woman gave up trying to attract the cleaner's attention. The terrible noise was growing louder. Something was crashing through the dense forest that bordered the car park. She whirled round and her eyes widened in horror.

3

Then she ran.

With an almighty roar, a huge creature burst from between the trees and pounded towards her. It was bigger than a rhino, with small, beady eyes, powerful legs and clawed feet. Evil-looking sabre teeth glinted in the pale lamplight. The beast paused for only a moment before thundering after its prey.

The woman hurled herself between two parked cars. Crash! One car was sent cartwheeling across the car park. She rolled underneath the second vehicle and out the other side, just in time. A split second later, the car crumpled beneath the animal's colossal weight. Then it was chasing her once more.

In desperation, the woman grabbed a hub cap from one of the wrecked cars and hurled it like a Frisbee. The beast stopped, distracted by the shiny disc of metal flashing in the light. It was just the chance she needed. The woman hurtled towards the edge of the car park, vanishing into the dark forest beyond. Behind her, the creature realized that its quarry had slipped away and roared its frustration to the dark skies.

Inside the supermarket, the cleaner continued mopping.

He saw nothing.

CHAPTER 1

Eight years later . . .

Professor Cutter walked briskly through the university campus. Lean and laid-back, he was far too good-looking to be a lecturer. Beside him was a young man with dark hair and soulful eyes – his trusty lab assistant, Stephen Hart. Their destination was the Department of Evolutionary Zoology.

'Professor Cutter!'

A student stumbled eagerly towards them, his progress hampered by a bag of very heavy books. He had a likeable face, unruly hair and the pasty complexion of a man who avoided exercise. In his haste, he tripped, scattering books across the ground. Bending to retrieve them, he looked up at Cutter awkwardly.

'Connor Temple, Professor,' he gasped.

'Never heard of it,' said Cutter absent-mindedly.

The student rolled his eyes. 'It's not a place,' he said. 'It's my name. I'm one of your students.'

'Really?' asked Cutter. 'Why don't I recognize you?'

'You never turn up for our seminars,' said Connor.

Stephen grinned. Knowing the professor as he did, this sounded a totally reasonable explanation.

Cutter sighed and gestured for Connor to follow them.

Although it looked out on to a busy laboratory, Cutter's office was an oasis of untidy calm. Pictures of ancient and modern animals plastered the walls. Books and papers were stacked on every available surface. And on the desk was a photo of an earnest-looking woman with long dark hair and fine features.

Cutter opened his canvas sack and produced a fossil. 'Tell me what this is,' he said to Connor.

'A fish?' the student replied uncertainly.

The professor sighed. 'Obviously,' he said. 'It's a Sarcopterygian – lobed, finned fish. No trace of them in the fossil record for seventy million years and then suddenly one pops up in the Indian Ocean. Totally inexplicable in traditional evolutionary terms.' He paused and looked at the fossil fondly. 'Darwin provides most of the answers. It's the pieces that don't fit that interest me.'

Connor's expression brightened at once. 'That's why I was wondering if you'd seen this.' He produced a sheaf of crumpled newsprint with the headline: MONSTER HOAX OR TRULY BEASTLY? Beneath was a grainy photograph. 'It looks like the real thing to me,' the student continued. 'Some kind of giant undiscovered predator.'

Cutter smiled kindly. 'It's a blatant hoax dreamt up for newspaper silly season. Forget it.' The subject closed, he returned his attention to the fossil, running his fingers along the ancient patterns in the stone.

But Connor wasn't going to give up this easily. He said the one thing that he knew would get the professor's attention. 'Your wife wouldn't have ignored something like this.'

Startled, Cutter looked at the photo on his desk, his eyes lingering on the image of the beautiful woman. 'My wife was a serious scientist,' he said coldly, 'not some gullible monster hunter.'

'I just thought you might want to check it out, that's all,' said the student quietly, aware that he was treading on thin ice. 'It's not as though the Forest of Dean is that far away.'

'The Forest of Dean . . .?' breathed Cutter.

CHAPTER 2

Abby Maitland sat observing her beloved Tuatara lizards. Young and pretty, what she didn't know about lizards wasn't worth knowing. She looked up as her boss, Tim Parker, entered the Reptile House, her smile fading as she saw his grim face.

'Abby, I'm sorry,' said Tim. 'The sponsors have pulled out. I have to slim down the reptile programme.'

Abby scowled. 'And my job comes under the heading of instant weight loss, right?'

Tim nodded, looking uncomfortable. 'There's an attachment going at the Bug House,' he said hopefully. 'I could put in a word for you.'

Her heart sank. 'I'm a lizard girl,' Abby said. 'You know that.'

Her boss's mobile rang, and as Tim answered it the stack of papers under his arm began to slide, cascading across the floor. He retreated to a corner to continue his conversation, while Abby picked up a jumbled mass of files. At once, she spotted a photograph of a boy aged about eleven. He was cradling an oddly beautiful lizard with a thin body, large head and enormous eyes. Instantly, her miserable expression turned to one of amazement.

Tim finished his call and came over to her. 'Letters from people asking the zoo to collect their animals,' he explained, pointing to the papers. He sighed. 'If they don't want exotic pets, why do they buy them?'

Abby's eyes were fixed on the photo. She didn't hear a word. And, in less time than it takes a Tuatara lizard to eat its lunch, she was on her way to investigate.

The walls of Ben Trent's room were plastered with pictures of Stegosaurus, Diplodocus and T-rex, to name but a few.

Abby stared round in wonderment. 'I see you like dinosaurs,' she said to the boy.

'They're awesome!' he replied.

Her eyes wandered over to the cage in the corner of the room. Inside was the lizard she recognized from the photo.

'I found him in the forest,' said Ben. 'His name's

Rex. I looked him up in a book – it said he was a flying dragon from South-East Asia.'

'Draco volans,' Abby said automatically, gazing at Rex in wonder and disbelief. Then she corrected herself. 'He's not Draco volans. In fact, I don't know what he is.'

Ben looked disappointed. 'I thought you were an expert.'

'I am,' replied Abby. 'If I'm right,' she said, 'you've discovered a completely unique species.' She took a breath, trying hard to control her excitement. 'I need you to show me exactly where you found him.'

Ten minutes later, Abby and Ben were wading through thick undergrowth, moving further and further into the dark and gloomy Forest of Dean.

Abby had wrapped the strange lizard in a scarf and held him close. 'It's too cold for him here,' she said. 'He must have escaped from a local zoo or something . . .'

Ben glanced at his watch and pulled a face. 'Mum'll go mental if I'm not home in time for tea,' he said. Then, abruptly, he stopped and pointed upwards. 'Abby . . .?' he said, his voice wavering.

Abby stared in horror. High above their heads,

10

half-hidden in the branches of a tall tree, hung the carcass of a dead cow. She gulped. It was a sight so surreal and so utterly sinister that it made her stomach churn.

A second later, a menacing growl echoed through the forest.

CHAPTER 3

Professor Cutter, Stephen and Connor had reached the Forest of Dean industrial park – a glum, soulless place at the edge of town. The only things that occupied it were huge metal containers that were stored here before being whisked away to far-off places.

But one container wasn't going anywhere. It was a wreck – ripped from top to bottom. Whoever – or whatever – had torn it open had been desperate to get inside.

'Can you imagine how much force it took to rip this thing open?' Connor exclaimed. 'Look at these marks! If you want my opinion . . .' His voice faltered as he met the professor's steely stare. 'Oh,' he mumbled. 'You don't.'

Cutter flicked his eyes towards Stephen, who was clearly puzzled.

The lab technician ran his fingertips over the scratches that scored the metal on either side of the jagged tear. 'If I'd found these scratches in the wild, I'd be certain we were searching for a very large predator,' he said softly.

'A wildcat, maybe?' suggested Cutter. 'Or an escaped panther?'

Keen to join in, Connor squeezed between the two men. 'Look at the size of that gash!' he said enthusiastically. 'Unless it's a panther with a serious steroid habit, you can forget it.'

Cutter ignored him. 'All right,' he said decisively. 'Someone ripped open the container with a forklift. Later, a wild boar or a big cat came foraging for food.'

Stephen touched a rust-coloured stain high up on the jagged metal. 'Blood,' he said simply.

'All right,' said Cutter, with a sigh. 'Give me a logical explanation.'

'A hoax, obviously,' said the lab technician. 'But difficult to pull off.'

As they spoke, Connor was jiggling with excitement. 'Can I say something?' he butted in.

Cutter glared at him, before striding away to stare moodily into the nearby forest.

Taking pity on the confused student, Stephen explained. 'Helen Cutter came to this area eight years ago,' he said quietly. 'She was investigating a

13

creature sighting – a large reptile. She disappeared in the forest. No blood, no clues, nothing. She simply vanished.' He paused for a moment. 'When he lost her, he lost a part of himself.'

That evening, Cutter went for a drink at the hotel bar. He didn't want company and was pleased to see that the place was deserted except for a beautiful woman in a smart suit, who was talking to a fat businessman. Suddenly, she rose elegantly to her feet and came to sit beside Cutter. To his total astonishment, she gave him a long kiss.

'Don't panic,' she muttered under her breath. 'I told Slimeball over there that you were my boyfriend.' She smiled at the businessman, who slunk back to his booth.

'Glad I was here to help,' said the professor wryly. 'Nick Cutter.'

'Actually,' said the woman, 'I know who you are.' She smiled at his startled face and introduced herself. 'Claudia Brown – Home Office. I'm hoping you can do me a favour, Professor.'

Cutter raised an eyebrow. 'Another one?'

Grinning, Claudia gestured to the barman for drinks. Then she opened her briefcase and pulled out

14

a series of familiar grainy photographs. 'I suspect this is why we're both here,' she said.

'Why should the Home Office be interested?' Cutter asked slowly.

'There are dozens of rogue animal reports every year,' the woman explained. 'Someone has to check them out and liaise with the local police.' She stopped and smiled. 'You'd be doing me a great service if you could just confirm that this is all nonsense.'

'I can't dismiss the evidence out of hand,' replied Cutter, suddenly suspicious of Claudia's motives.

'Surely you're not giving this monster story any credibility?' she said.

Cutter chose his words carefully. 'It depends on how you define "monster",' he said. 'A wild panther might look pretty terrifying on a dark night.' He glanced at his watch. 'Whatever it was, the last sighting was near the forest. Care to join the search?'

'I suppose I owe it to the taxpayer to do more than sit in my room sucking the minibar dry,' she said, with a grin. As they left the bar, she merrily waved the businessman goodbye.

Connor and Stephen were waiting in the hotel car park.

'This database contains constantly updated information on all known extinct vertebrates,' Connor said, pointing proudly to his laptop. 'I've been building it every spare minute since I was fourteen.'

'Impressive,' drawled Stephen. 'And slightly sad.'

Connor spoke in a low, confidential tone. 'You know we're not talking about a wildcat, don't you?' he said.

At this, Stephen looked suddenly unsure. But before he could reply, Cutter appeared with the woman from the hotel bar.

'This is Claudia Brown from the Home Office,' he introduced her.

Connor exploded with indignation. 'It's a cover-up. I knew it!' he shouted.

Professor Cutter smiled at Claudia. 'Connor never met a conspiracy theory that he didn't like,' he said.

CHAPTER 4

Something large rustled through the undergrowth, cracking foliage underfoot. Abby and Ben stared at each other nervously as the noise faded away.

'How does a dead cow get up a tree?' whispered the boy.

'There's probably a perfectly simple explanation,' said Abby, sounding unconvincing even to herself.

Ben shivered uneasily. 'Some predators take their prey up into the trees and come back for it later,' he said.

'There's no predator alive that could do that with a cow, Ben,' said Abby. If there was one thing she was sure of, it was that.

'Look, I found Rex round here somewhere,' said Ben, swiftly changing the subject. 'Can we go home now?' An ominous shadow flitted between the trees. 'What was that?' he breathed.

At once, the chilling growl echoed through the

forest again, this time much closer. Ben stared at Abby with wide, frightened eyes, before turning on his heel and running helter-skelter back the way they'd come.

'Ben!' cried Abby. She raced after him, but Rex chose that moment to wriggle out of her arms and shoot off into the undergrowth. Abby stumbled to a halt, torn between the exotic lizard and the disappearing boy. 'Ben . . . wait!' she called, before diving under the bushes where Rex had vanished. There he was, staring at her solemnly from beneath the thick leaves. She reached towards the lizard and spoke, her voice pleading. 'Not now, Rex. Please, come back.'

The lizard moved towards Abby. Then, neck stretched and eyes alert, he froze.

'Rex?' said Abby. 'What's wrong?'

A second later, the bushes around her trembled and the earth began to vibrate. She looked round in astonishment as the sound of a heavy body crashing through undergrowth filled the air. The terrifying creature stopped so close that Abby could see its huge reptilian legs and feet. Then, without warning, it thundered away, the bushes shielding its massive body from view.

Rigid with terror, Abby dared to breathe again. Then, remembering Ben, she looked around frantically for the boy.

He was nowhere to be seen.

Torchlight sliced through the darkness. Map in hand, Stephen led the way. Connor followed close behind, consulting his compass, while Cutter and Claudia brought up the rear.

'If there really were some creature here, wouldn't the journalists have found it by now?' Claudia reasoned.

Cutter shrugged. 'They have no idea what they're looking for,' he said. 'Even if they did, they wouldn't know how to go about finding it.'

'But you do?' asked Claudia.

'I've seen Stephen track a wounded animal through the rainforest for ten days at a time,' was the professor's reply.

Claudia studied him thoughtfully. 'Your wife went missing somewhere near here, didn't she?' she asked.

Instantly, the professor stiffened. 'Is that relevant?' he said, his voice hard.

She raised her eyebrows. 'Just wondering what the

real agenda is –' But before Claudia could finish her sentence, an unearthly growl pierced the gloom.

At once, the small party stopped dead.

Stephen shone the torch around them, noticing that nearby foliage had been disturbed and low branches snapped. And then he looked upwards, his eyes resting on a point above them. Immediately, he nudged Cutter, who followed his gaze to the dead cow, still suspended in the high branches.

But something else was puzzling Connor. 'Professor?' he called, his eyes wide and confused. He held out the compass in utter bewilderment.

The needle was spinning around like crazy.

CHAPTER 5

Ben ran in panic from the monster, stumbling over rough ground and forcing his way through spiky undergrowth. His breathing was ragged with terror. Up ahead, he saw the trees thinning. He must have reached the edge of the forest at last. He was safe now. But then he realized that it was just a clearing.

Ben gulped. A strange, flickering light shone from between the trees. Slowly, he moved closer. There was a mysterious disturbance in the air, almost as if a gash had been gouged there. Glittering shards of light danced all around.

It was beautiful.

His fear momentarily forgotten, Ben walked over to the light and reached out to touch it. He gasped in awe as his hand disappeared, then hesitated for a moment before popping his head into the rippling air . . . In every direction, there was nothing but sand and rock. He was in the middle of a desert – a prehistoric desert. The sun was huge in the sky and it was baking hot, totally unlike the cold, dark, gloomy forest. Suddenly, a flock of flying lizards just like Rex zipped by, millimetres from his nose. Ben gasped in amazement and pulled his head back sharply . . . into the forest.

Wow!

Ben caught his breath. Then he grinned with excitement. He'd seen another world beyond the forest – another world, another time! Wait until he told his mates about this. They'd be so impressed. He was just about to jump right into the mysterious desert when he heard an unmistakeable growl in the distance.

Ben didn't hang about. The desert could wait. Right now, he needed to get out of here.

The boy dodged between the trees, catching his clothes on stray branches and tripping over rocks. He ran on and on until – at long last – he reached the edge of the forest. His pace slackened as he neared exhaustion. He knew he couldn't run for much longer. Suddenly, he saw lights in the distance and hurtled down the hill towards the road – and home.

As Ben vaulted the fence that bordered his garden, he grazed his hand on the wire. Sucking the bleeding wound quickly, he rushed to his house and opened the door, crashing it shut behind him.

Inside the house, Ben thundered up the stairs and into his room, slamming the door and leaning against it. He was safe.

'Ben?' called his mother anxiously. 'Where have you been?'

He didn't have enough breath to answer. With a huge sense of relief, he slumped on his bunk bed, his back to the window.

Slowly, majestically, a huge sabre-toothed head rose into sight outside the window. Eyes glinting wickedly, it stared into the boy's bedroom. Then a shaft of moonlight revealed the Gorgonopsid in all its fearsome glory. A savage predator, the beast was like a rhino, only larger. Its head was massive, with razor-sharp canines, tiny eyes and holes for ears. And it was separated from its prey by only a single pane of glass.

Ben felt a prickling sensation on the skin at the back of his neck. He was being watched – he knew it. Slowly, oh so slowly, he turned until he was eyeball-to-eyeball with a beast from his worst nightmares.

For a split second, boy and creature simply stared at each other.

Then all hell broke loose.

The Gorgonopsid's huge front claw smashed through the glass and grabbed at Ben. He leapt up like a jack-in-the-box, just as the monstrous creature jammed its head through the broken window, teeth bared in a ferocious snarl. Ben scrambled backwards, to the far end of his bed. But the animal lashed out, catching the bunk. One end of the bed collapsed, sending the boy sliding down towards the Gorgonopsid's hungry mouth.

Frantically, Ben clung to the top of the bed with one hand, using his free hand to hurl anything within his grasp into the creature's face. Then, just as he began to lose his grip, he spotted his glass globe by the bedside. He lunged for it, then threw the globe right at the animal.

He scored a direct hit. The glass exploded into thousands of tiny pieces, sending the startled creature reeling back. It flailed furiously, then lost its balance and dropped out of sight.

Crash! The bedroom door ricocheted against the wall.

This time, it wasn't the Gorgonopsid. But it was someone equally scary.

'What on earth is going on in here?' demanded Mrs Trent. She slowly surveyed the smashed window and overturned furniture before turning back to her trembling son. 'Right, young man,' she said. 'I want an explanation for this mess. Now.'

CHAPTER 6

Abby spun round desperately, lost in the maze of trees.

'OK, Rex,' she muttered nervously to the creature cradled in her arms. 'Which way?'

She moved forward a couple of paces, before freezing at the sound of heavy, shuffling footsteps. Rex sniffed the air suspiciously. Terrified, Abby looked behind her. Seeing nothing, she turned back –

'Arrggghhhhh!' she screamed as she crashed headlong into the most monstrous beast she'd ever seen. It was about three metres long with short, thick growths protruding from its gargoyle head. Very heavy upfront, it had a short tail and stumpy back legs. Its leathery hide was dotted with knobbly ridges.

Abby dropped Rex and staggered back in horror. But instead of ripping her to shreds, the monster stared at her with gentle, cow-like eyes before bending down to munch at the shrubs dotted around its feet.

Suddenly, a torch beam pierced the darkness and Abby blinked in its glare.

'Don't move,' hissed a man's voice.

It was Professor Cutter. He and his team appeared from between the trees. And as they did so, the animal backed away warily.

Abby looked around in confusion. 'What's going on?'

'Some kind of experiment, maybe,' Cutter mused, his eyes fixed on the huge creature. 'A hybrid or throwback . . .' He paused before switching his attention to Abby. 'Who are you?'

'Abby Maitland,' she said, trying to keep calm. 'I'm a keeper at Wellington Zoo.'

'What do you know about this?' asked Cutter.

'Nothing . . .' said Abby. Her voice trembled as she spoke.

Stephen gave her an encouraging smile. 'It's OK,' he said. 'You're safe now.'

'How do you know?' asked Abby.

Stephen shrugged. She had a point.

By now, Cutter's curiosity had overcome his shock. He circled the beast, talking quietly to himself. 'Reptilian . . . four to five tonnes at least . . . large supratemporal bosses . . . huge osteoderms on its

27

back.' He stood back. 'Must be some kind of anapsid,' he concluded.

'A tortoise?' scoffed Abby. 'You've got to be kidding!' As Cutter disappeared behind the beast, she noticed it becoming increasingly restless. 'Stay in his field of vision,' she told him. 'You're making him nervous.'

Cutter looked startled, but nevertheless did as he was told. Instantly, the creature became calmer.

Abby smiled. 'Rhinos are just the same,' she said.

Claudia had been eagerly watching the proceedings. Now she could keep quiet no longer. 'Correct me if I'm wrong,' she began, 'but this creature shouldn't exist?'

'Obviously not,' said Cutter infuriatingly.

'Then why is it standing right in front of me?' demanded the woman from the Home Office, just as Connor held up his mobile and took a photo.

The flash surprised the animal, making it rear back, lowing in distress.

At once, Claudia whipped the phone from Connor's hand and quickly deleted the photo. 'Whatever it is,' she snapped, 'it's classified until I find out what to do about it.' She tossed the mobile back to the speechless student.

Abby calmed the anxious beast, which responded to her gentle reassurance immediately.

Cutter was impressed. And that was when he noticed Rex sitting in the grass.

Stephen followed his gaze. 'Crikey,' he said. 'There's two of them.'

'A local boy found him nearby . . .' explained Abby, her voice failing as the horrible truth dawned. 'Oh no!' she cried. 'Ben!'

It didn't take long for the group of three to reach the Trents' house. While Abby and Cutter made sure that Ben was OK, Claudia hung back to use her mobile.

'No, I can't use the police,' she said urgently. 'This is too sensitive. Now get someone down here, fast.' She turned off the phone, took a deep breath and went inside.

Professor Cutter and Abby were speaking to Ben and his mother.

'I'll be making a complaint,' said Mrs Trent crossly. 'She's filled his head with all sorts of stupid ideas. Look at the state of his room!' Angrily, she pointed at the chaos.

'It was the monster!' cried Ben. 'Tell them, Abby –'

Cutter butted in. 'The simple truth is that Miss Maitland got carried away,' he lied calmly. 'Ben's pet was nothing more exotic than Draco volans, the South-East Asian flying lizard. I'm afraid your son has been lost in the woods during this adventure.'

'It was a monster,' Ben said, stubbornly sticking to his story. 'Tell them, Abby.'

Abby raised her head to find that Claudia Brown's intense gaze was fixed on her. She hesitated before guiltily muttering her response. 'I don't really know what happened, Ben,' she said. 'We got frightened, that's all.'

'But I saw the past!' the boy insisted. 'Prehistoric times! I was there!'

'You saw the past?' asked Cutter.

'I was standing right in it,' said Ben. 'There was a desert, rocks and things . . .'

His mother sighed. 'I blame the telly,' she said. 'They make it all seem so real that the kids start believing there's a dinosaur round every corner.'

Moments later, Cutter, Claudia and a very guilty-looking Abby stood on the pavement outside the Trents' house.

'I know you feel bad about lying,' Claudia said

sympathetically to Abby, 'but who knows what the consequences might have been if you'd told the truth.' She regarded them with a serious expression. 'You're both going to have to sign the Official Secrets Act.'

Cutter raised his eyebrows. 'Since when did this become an official secret?'

'About ten minutes after I finally persuaded my boss not to have me sectioned,' Claudia replied. 'You try telling a senior civil servant to put the SAS on monster alert.'

The professor smiled, but his expression quickly grew thoughtful. 'Right now, we have a more urgent problem,' he said seriously. 'That creature we saw may be many things, but it's certainly not a ruthless predator that drags its prey up into trees.'

'You can't be sure of that,' Claudia said.

'He can,' said Abby. 'It's a herbivore. Pure veggie.'

The woman from the Home Office went pale. 'You mean there's another one out there?'

Cutter nodded, but already his mind was elsewhere. 'What did Ben mean when he talked about seeing the past?' He looked uneasy, before adding thoughtfully, 'These animals have to be coming from somewhere . . .'

'What are you saying?' Claudia asked.

The professor paused before replying. 'I'm saying the answer is out there in that forest – and maybe Ben found it.'

Connor and Stephen were still watching the strange beast.

'You know this is going to win me the Nobel Prize?' Connor said, wearing a look of dreamy self-satisfaction.

Stephen rolled his eyes. 'We don't know what we're dealing with yet,' he reminded the student.

'Come on,' said Connor. 'It looks like a dinosaur. It behaves like a dinosaur. It's a dinosaur – a missing link to the ancient past. And I discovered it.'

'What about the rest of us?' asked Stephen.

'Don't worry,' replied Connor, smiling generously. 'I won't forget the little people.'

It was at this moment that the animal stopped grazing and began to amble away.

'Where's it going?' asked Connor bleakly, watching its departure in dismay. 'Stop it!' he told Stephen.

'You stop it,' said Stephen, not moving a muscle.

An urgent shout interrupted them.

'Let it go!' called Cutter. He appeared through

the trees with Claudia and Abby. 'It's frightened,' he puffed. 'Let's see where it thinks it's safe.'

They chased after the beast, crashing through the forest, pushing aside branches and tripping over the undergrowth.

Suddenly, they found themselves in the clearing that Ben had discovered. The beast plunged towards the glittering shards of light. In seconds, it had vanished into sparkling air.

'Where did it go?' whispered Claudia.

'Home,' said the professor simply.

CHAPTER 7

Early the next morning, the official government response began. The clearing was cordoned off and, inside the flimsy barrier, there was a frenzy of activity. Scientists scurried to and fro, their progress hampered by military personnel unloading weaponry.

Abby sat by a nearby tree, her fingers closing gratefully round the coffee that Stephen handed to her.

'How are you feeling?' he asked.

'Confused,' said Abby. 'Frightened. Exhilarated.'

'Snap.'

They smiled at each other, before hurriedly looking away.

Connor was very pleased with himself. While gazing in awe at the rippling fault in the air, he'd accidentally dropped his metal pen. Rather than tumbling to the ground, it had flown towards the anomaly – as the scientists had chosen to call it – disappearing with a faint pop of energy. 'That explains the compass,' he said proudly, remembering how the dial had spun the day before.

Now Cutter was interested. 'What could cause a magnetic field so powerful?' he wondered, watching as the student aimed more and more objects at the disturbance.

'Oh,' said Connor. 'That was my front-door key.'

Cutter rolled his eyes.

'You said that the creature had gone home,' Claudia said to the professor. 'All right, I'll buy it. Where's home?'

This was something that Cutter did know about. 'Everything about the animals we've seen so far is consistent with vertebrates that last appeared in the fossil record hundreds of millions of years ago.'

'You mean they're like creatures from the past?' she said.

'I mean they are creatures from the past.'

Claudia's eyes opened wide. 'So . . . you really believe I could step through that . . . thing . . . and somehow go back millions of years in time?'

'There's only one sure way to find out,' replied Cutter.

She shivered, before turning businesslike once more. 'The Home Office brainiacs are on their way,' she said. 'Maybe they'll find out more. We have to go now.'

'I'm not going anywhere,' said Cutter. 'There's a dangerous predator on the loose.'

'I need your help,' Claudia said urgently.

Cutter didn't budge. 'You've got your own experts.'

'They didn't see what we saw,' she replied. 'And they don't know what you know.' She walked away before the professor could argue.

Frustrated, Cutter turned back towards the glittering phenomenon.

Stephen joined him. 'You're thinking that Helen went through,' he said softly.

Cutter nodded. 'It explains everything.'

'Except why she didn't come back,' said Stephen. 'It was eight years ago. Even if you're right, she couldn't still be –' Abruptly, he stopped, but they both knew what he'd been about to say.

Alive.

Lester stared disdainfully through the two-way mirror. Inside the interview room, Cutter and Abby were being questioned by the secret services. He sighed. This was all he needed – a bunch of scientific busybodies and a forest full of supposedly extinct creatures. He smoothed his hands over his pinstriped suit, looking up as a smartly dressed woman approached.

'Claudia Brown,' she introduced herself. 'Home Office. I'll be working for you on this case.'

'Yes,' he said snootily, ignoring her outstretched hand. 'I've seen your file. James Lester. I'll be in charge of coordinating our response.' He turned back to the interview room. 'You shouldn't have brought them with you. They have no security clearance. I don't like civilians in these situations.'

Claudia raised an eyebrow. 'Professor Cutter's qualifications speak for themselves,' she said calmly. 'And the girl is a reptile specialist.'

Lester shook his head in tired disbelief. 'You spend your entire career making contingency plans for just about any crisis imaginable, up to and including alien invasion, and then this happens,' he said.

As soon as the interview was over, Cutter and Abby found themselves trailing after Claudia and the increasingly grumpy Lester through the glass and metal maze of the Home Office building. They reached a laboratory with glass walls and stopped outside.

'Where's Rex?' asked Abby. The reptile had been whisked away from her as soon as she'd arrived and she was beginning to worry about him.

Lester tried to smile reassuringly. 'He's quite safe.' He turned back to Cutter. 'This . . . phenomenon, Professor. Claudia tells me you have an explanation.'

'A theory,' Cutter corrected him. 'The boy's experience proves there's a concrete landscape on the other side of the anomaly. I think it's the Earth, many millions of years ago.'

'This anomaly, as you call it, is a door between time zones in the world's history?'

Cutter nodded.

'Suppose your theory is correct . . .' said Lester. 'What are the immediate risks?'

The professor looked at him in exasperation. Did he really need to spell it out? Seeing Lester's expression, it appeared that he did. 'Famine, war, pestilence, the end of the world as we know it,' he said, before suddenly exploding with anger at the sheer ludicrousness of this conversation. 'I could do without standing in a corridor in Whitehall talking to a civil service pen-pusher when I should be exploring the most significant phenomenon in the history of science!'

He and Lester locked eyes – Cutter bristling with fury, while Lester was icily calm.

'Technically, I'm not a civil servant,' Lester said coolly. 'More troubleshooting without portfolio in the PM's office.'

'A government hatchet man,' said Cutter.

'Colourful,' Lester replied, 'but surprisingly accurate.'

Cutter took a deep breath, mustering all his patience. 'The risks are incalculable,' he explained. 'Creature incursion, modern viruses polluting the primitive environment, decisive changes in evolutionary development . . . And there's one thing you should know. I intend to find out what happened to my wife, whatever the risks. I'm going through the anomaly. If you want to stop me, you'll have to shoot me.'

'Let's hope it doesn't come to that,' Lester said dryly.

CHAPTER 8

Stephen and Connor tramped through the Forest of Dean, examining the flattened foliage.

'So . . . what do you think of Abby?' Connor asked awkwardly.

'She's OK,' replied Stephen. 'Why?'

'Do you think she liked me?'

Stephen shrugged. 'Why don't you ask her yourself?' he said, avoiding the question.

'I might,' said Connor. 'It's not every day you meet a potential girlfriend and find a dinosaur.'

The lab technician didn't reply, bending down towards the forest floor instead. There, in a patch of sticky mud, was a huge reptilian footprint. He gestured urgently to Connor, who rushed over. Together, they stared at the footprint with growing unease.

'What is it?' asked Stephen.

Connor turned even paler than usual. 'I think the scientific term is Really Bad News,' he said, delving into his rucksack and pulling out his trusty laptop. He trawled quickly through his database, looking increasingly nervous. 'My best guess is that the creature we found was some kind of Scutosaurus. Late Permian era. Two hundred and fifty million years ago, give or take a week.' He looked at the footprint again and compared it with the images flashing past on his computer screen. 'This footprint definitely doesn't come from the same animal. If we're talking Permian, this little charmer is the prime suspect.'

Stephen leaned closer to look at the laptop.

'The Gorgonopsid,' said Connor. 'One of the most lethal predators ever known. Stupid and bad-tempered. A compact killing machine of incredible power. If it's still out there, you have to find it. Fast.'

'Me?' said Stephen. 'What about you?'

Connor grinned. 'You, mighty hunter,' he said. 'Me, logistics and backup.'

Abby looked through the glass wall in dismay as the Home Office scientists examined her beloved Rex. 'They shouldn't handle a lizard like that,' she muttered, wincing with every poke and prod. 'He's frightened.'

'Let the experts do their job,' sighed Lester.

Honestly, even if it was prehistoric, it was only a lizard.

'But they don't know what they're doing,' said Abby, watching as Rex was plonked on the table of an MRI scanner. The little creature hissed angrily. 'Do they even know he can fly?' she asked.

'Fly?' asked Lester.

At that moment, three things happened: a scientist opened the door to the forensic lab; the MRI belt whirred into life; and Rex decided that he'd had enough of being a specimen. He spread his scaly wings wide and took off, hurtling at astonishing speed through the open door and zooming along the corridor. In seconds, he'd vanished.

'Rex!' cried Abby, racing after him.

But Rex was free. He dodged, ducked and dived his way through the huge building until he reached an open window on an upper floor. He landed gracefully on the window ledge, staring at the outside world with huge, uncomprehending eyes. In a second, he would be gone.

Gasping for breath, Abby and Cutter skidded to a halt a few feet away.

'Don't do it, Rex!' Abby whispered urgently. Cautiously, she drew closer, and thought quickly. It was a long shot, but it might work . . . She reached into her pocket and pulled out a bar of chocolate, snapping off a small piece and offering it to Rex. 'Trust me,' she said. 'You're going to love it.'

Rex stared at the blue sky and then back at the chocolate. To everyone's dismay, he spread his wings and took off, but then at the very last second he veered away from the window and headed back to Abby. The little lizard landed on her arm and licked at the chocolate.

'Good decision, Rex,' said Abby softly. 'It's not your world out there any more.'

Sighing with relief, Cutter glanced at Lester. Then he began to smile. 'Those risks you were asking about,' said the professor. 'That's one I forgot.' And he pointed to the splodge of prehistoric green goo that was trickling slowly down the government official's pristine suit.

Lester reappeared a few moments later, his angry face daring anyone to make fun of his little mishap. He got straight down to business. 'The lizard's DNA appears to confirm your theory,' he said to Cutter. 'The creature is a living fossil. Given the circumstances, I'm going to allow your exploratory mission into the anomaly.'

This was unexpected. 'What changed your mind?' asked Cutter.

'I'm not insensitive to your personal situation,' said the official. 'And the bonus is that you're well qualified to analyse what you see.'

'I'm taking the lizard,' said Cutter quickly. 'Creatures that don't belong here should be returned to their original habitat.'

Lester nodded and slid a document across the table. 'It's a disclaimer,' he explained. 'We don't want any nasty lawsuits if you don't come back.'

Without hesitation, Cutter signed on the dotted line.

When they'd left, Lester took out his mobile and made a call. 'It's done,' he said. 'If he comes back, we'll know exactly what we're dealing with. If not, we've solved a potential problem.' He smiled grimly. 'I'd say that was a win–win situation.'

Ben stared out of the tall, classroom window at the playing fields and the wood beyond. It was after school, and he was the only student left. He was supposed to be concentrating on his lines, only Ben couldn't think about anything but the dinosaur that had attacked him in his bedroom. Would anyone ever believe him?

The sound of his teacher's voice made him jump. 'The sooner you finish your detention,' she said, 'the sooner we can both go home.'

A tiny flicker out of the corner of his eye alerted Ben. He swivelled his head to see the mighty Gorgonopsid stalking past the window. At once, he rocketed to his feet, pale with terror. 'Miss!' he cried. 'There's a dinosaur in the playground!'

The teacher rolled her eyes. 'Really, Ben,' she said. 'How old are you? Sit down, now!'

*

The Gorgonopsid slipped through the main entrance, crouching slightly because of its vast bulk. It padded down corridor after corridor, peering into empty classrooms as it went.

Thud!

Hearing a noise in the corridor, the teacher got up to investigate.

'Don't open the door, Miss!' warned Ben, terrified now. He watched as a huge shadow appeared behind the glass. 'Don't open it!'

The teacher paused for a split-second, her hand on the door handle . . . And then she pulled it wide open, to see the Gorgonopsid leering down at her. Screaming, she slammed the door in its face, leaning against the wood as it trembled with the angry dinosaur's onslaught. The door splintered, but held – just.

'I told you not to open it!' wailed Ben.

The Gorgonopsid flung itself repeatedly against the door, as the teacher and Ben frantically tried to barricade themselves in, but –

Crash!

The classroom door burst inwards, revealing the dinosaur in all its fearsome glory. It opened its great jaws wide and roared so loudly that the room trembled.

Ben and his teacher scrambled backwards, away from the monster, desperately flinging books in a vain attempt to halt its progress. It advanced, furious.

Doink!

A bright orange basketball zoomed through the air and bounced off the enormous creature's head. It turned in confusion.

'Hey!' shouted Stephen. 'Pick on someone your own size!'

It hadn't taken him long to follow the Gorgonopsid's trail through the Forest of Dean and to the school. Now he saw that it was up to him to save the boy and his teacher. Taking a deep breath, Stephen hurled another ball at the monster's head. Then he sped away.

Enraged, the dinosaur thundered after him, stumbling over the obstacles – tables, bookcases, desks – that the lab technician pushed into its path.

Stephen sprinted onwards, satisfied that the dinosaur was following the human bait. It thundered after him, chasing him down endless corridors until he reached a dead end. Luckily, there was a fire door up ahead – a way out.

It was locked.

The beast reared above Stephen, roaring in triumph, its jaws opening to slice him in two . . . But at the last second, Stephen leapt to one side, grabbed a fire extinguisher from the wall and sprayed it right in the dinosaur's face. It lurched back in panic and there was silence. Then, infuriated and half-blinded, the beast charged again, bursting open the fire door and flinging Stephen out of the building.

The young man crashed to the ground and was still.

CHAPTER 10

Huge floodlights bleached all colour from the clearing. Scientists were carefully analysing data while the SAS stood guard. There was a tense excitement in the air.

Cutter stood in the midst of a group of scientists, who fussed over him like mother hens. Claudia and Connor watched anxiously from the sidelines.

'The predator's still out there somewhere,' Cutter said under his breath. 'Call Stephen again.'

'He's not answering,' replied Connor.

'You've got enough to think about,' said Claudia in a soothing voice. 'Let us worry about the creature.'

Reluctantly, Cutter gave way. The anomaly was waiting for him – and who knew what was beyond.

Claudia checked her watch. 'It's 18:55. I want you back no later than 20:00 hours. If the first contact works out, we'll take it from there.'

The professor nodded. Then, as a burly soldier dressed in full battle gear approached, he looked at

49

Claudia in surprise. 'What's he doing?' he asked.

'Captain Ryan is a Gulf War veteran with extensive desert experience,' she said. 'No argument, Cutter. He goes as well.'

Cutter saw her determined expression and realized that he wouldn't change her mind. If that was the way they wanted to play it, he wouldn't argue. Just as long as they didn't stop him from reaching Helen – if she was there.

Abby walked towards him, holding Rex. 'Take care of him,' she said softly. 'And watch out for yourself too.' She smiled as she handed over the lizard. Impulsively, she hugged the professor.

Claudia spoke quietly to Ryan. 'Whatever happens, bring him back,' she said.

The soldier nodded.

Cutter took a deep, steadying breath. He was excited and terrified in equal measure. It was almost too much to take in. He was about to do what every scientist, every zoologist, surely every person in the world had always dreamt of doing. He was about to travel 200 million years into the past, when dinosaurs ruled the Earth . . .

Giving himself a shake, he glanced briskly at his watch. It was time. Together, he and Ryan walked towards the sparkling, swirling anomaly. The clearing went deathly quiet. Everyone was watching, horribly aware of the significance, the awe-inspiring strangeness and – above all – the danger of this mission.

The two men paused on the threshold of the glittering gateway. Edging forward, they were bathed in flickering light as the anomaly shivered with energy.

And then they vanished.

In the clearing, you could hear a pin drop. As Connor stared at the twinkling shards of light, his pen slipped from his fingers. It was only when he bent to pick it up that he realized what it meant.

'My pen!' he cried. 'The magnetic field didn't take it . . .' He looked at Claudia in horror. 'The anomaly's getting weaker.'

Cutter and Ryan emerged into a rocky landscape of shale and sand. They gazed around them, breathless at the speed of the transition between present and past.

The professor quickly checked his pulse. It was normal. 'Did you feel anything?' he asked the soldier.

Ryan shook his head.

In the fierce daylight, the anomaly was nearly

invisible. Ryan opened his rucksack and planted a marker so they'd find it again. Meanwhile, Cutter placed Rex carefully on the ground. The lizard paused quizzically for a second, then scurried between nearby rocks.

'At least someone's happy to be here,' said Ryan with a wry smile.

Cutter gazed around at the bleak landscape. He felt no fear, just a sense of wonder at this unbelievable view of the planet in its infancy. In many ways, it reminded him of the remote corners of present-day Earth – fresh mountain air, stunning scenery, a sense of space and calm – but in other ways it was totally different. Here, everything was raw, new, untouched . . . Stones were sharper, the sun was brighter and the air was so clear that distant mountains were razor-sharp. He wandered down into a valley and over a rise, not even sure what he was looking for. Now that he was actually here, the search for Helen seemed absurd.

And then he saw the dinosaurs.

Vast herds of prehistoric creatures were dotted about the hills, grazing like cows. Cutter felt suddenly privileged beyond belief to be here.

The professor had no idea how long he'd been staring at the curiously calming landscape when the soldier's voice interrupted his thoughts. 'You need to see this,' he called from the top of a nearby ridge.

Reluctantly, Cutter turned his back on the view and clambered up a scree of loose stones to reach Ryan. As the professor drew closer, he realized that the shapes in the sand were too precise and geometric to be natural. He wiped the sand off the nearest hillock and found himself staring at a camouflage net. Next, there were boxes, weapons, tents and radio sets. It was a military camp, abandoned long ago. Cutter prised the lid from a box and found tins of food stacked inside. The labels were all in English.

'Who were they?' he asked. 'Where did they go?'

Ryan gestured towards something in the sand nearby. 'Whoever it was, they didn't get very far,' he replied. It was a skeleton, a few tiny scraps of clothing still clinging to the bones. Beside the remains was a weather-beaten camera case.

With trembling hands, Cutter picked it up. Inside, the camera was perfectly intact. And engraved on the leather were two letters that made his heart turn over. 'HC,' he read aloud. 'Helen Cutter.'

'Is it her?' asked Ryan, staring back at the skeleton.

Cutter bent down to look. After a second, he shook

his head, overwhelmed with relief. 'It's a man,' he said.

'How did he die?'

The professor shrugged. He stood up and looked around helplessly at the huge, empty desert. Where was Helen? Lost in time?

The burly soldier glanced at his watch. 'Time to go,' he said briskly.

Cutter couldn't believe the hour they'd been allotted had gone so fast. And one thing was certain. He wasn't about to leave now. 'I'm staying,' he said calmly.

'My orders are that we go back together.'

'I can't help that,' said Cutter stubbornly. 'I'm going to find my wife.'

Ryan's reply was brief and blunt. 'Face it – she's dead.'

Cutter didn't even bother to reply. As he turned to go, Ryan picked up his gun. With one practised movement, the soldier brought the rifle butt down on the back of Cutter's neck. He groaned and sank to his knees.

'Sorry, Professor,' said Ryan, grabbing the unconscious man under the arms. It was time to get back to the anomaly.

Rex looked up curiously as the two men approached.

Ryan was half-carrying, half-dragging Cutter, who suddenly came to his senses and struggled to get away. As the soldier fought to restrain his charge, he scanned the area for the anomaly marker. There it was, just where they'd left it.

But the anomaly had disappeared.

CHAPTER 11

'Where's it gone?' Ryan cried.

All thoughts of fighting evaporated. Cutter followed the soldier's anxious gaze. It was true. Not even the smallest glimmer of light disturbed the still air.

And then, just as they had begun to think they were stuck in the prehistoric past, the anomaly reappeared, flickering feebly. Ryan rushed to the brink of it, feeling frantically in the air. When his arm vanished, the soldier knew that he'd found their escape route. 'Quick!' he yelled, staring wildly at Cutter, who hadn't moved. 'You want to be trapped here forever?' he cried.

The professor shrugged. 'Maybe it'll open again one day,' he said calmly. 'I'll find Helen and wait.'

But Ryan had made a promise to Claudia – and he wasn't about to break it. He stepped away from the anomaly. 'You stay,' he said grimly, crossing his arms, 'I stay.'

Cutter knew when he was beaten. It was one thing to risk his own life, but quite another to risk someone else's. 'All right,' he said reluctantly.

Together, they approached the anomaly. The glittering gateway flashed as Cutter hurled himself forward. A split second later, Ryan followed. Abruptly, the two men disappeared.

Rex watched them go. And then, just as the anomaly flickered with one final burst of energy, the little lizard swooped after them . . .

Back in the Forest of Dean, the anomaly began to shiver with movement. For a second, the outlines of two men were clearly visible. Then they began to fade. There was a moment of sickening tension before – almost reluctantly – the anomaly gave up its human cargo. Cutter and Ryan were flung clear just in time. Behind them, the anomaly consumed itself in a final burst of dazzling energy.

Immediately, the two men were engulfed by a crowd of well-wishers. But something made Abby hang back. She glanced at the place where the anomaly had been and saw a little creature that made her grin with delight. It was Rex. His return had gone unnoticed in the uproar. Quickly, she picked up the lizard and slipped him beneath her jacket.

CRASH!

The drama wasn't over yet. Without warning, the mighty Gorgonopsid had returned. It thundered through the clearing, smashing floodlights and scientific equipment underfoot in its desperate search for the way home. The SAS let loose a shower of bullets, but these pinged off the angry dinosaur's tough hide, serving only to infuriate it further.

Connor grabbed Abby's hand and dragged her to safety, but Claudia remained in the Gorgonopsid's path. He called her name but she was frozen by fear. Bravely, Cutter rushed out in front to distract the beast, but he tripped. Now both he and Claudia were at the creature's mercy. In a second, they would be ripped to pieces . . .

Suddenly, headlights glinted through the trees. An engine revved furiously and Cutter's four-by-four careered into the clearing, slamming into the dinosaur's rump. The Gorgonopsid was flung across the ground, before lying still. Shakily, Stephen climbed from behind the wheel. There was an eerie silence as he looked at the mighty creature.

But it wasn't over. With a strangled roar, the dinosaur hauled itself to its feet and stumbled towards him.

It was Cutter's turn to come to the rescue. He grabbed a gun and hurled it to Stephen, who caught it neatly – and fired right between the dinosaur's gaping jaws. The Gorgonopsid carried on towards him for a few more steps, before giving an ear-splitting roar and sinking to the ground, mortally wounded. With a last groan of pain and confusion, it died.

There was an atmosphere of stunned disbelief as people emerged from their hiding places. No one spoke. Sadly, Cutter walked over to the dead dinosaur and gently touched its great head.

CHAPTER 12

Cutter stared at the projector screen, even though the image of his wife had faded now.

'I'm sorry for your personal loss, Professor,' said Lester, his voice as unemotional as if he were ordering a takeaway. 'This camp you've discovered,' he continued. 'There were no clues who made it or what it was for?'

Cutter shook his head.

'The thought that someone has been there before us is far from reassuring,' Lester said thoughtfully. 'Clearly, we must remain on our guard.' He pulled a face. 'And I used to think the EU Common Agricultural Policy was far-fetched . . . Well, at least the immediate crisis is over.'

The professor could contain his anger no longer. This unimaginative government official still didn't get it. He whirled round to face Lester, his eyes blazing. 'Some force out there ripped the boundaries of time and space to shreds. Maybe it's happened before, in which case everything we thought we understood about the universe is wrong. Or perhaps this is the first time. But if so, what's changed? What happens next?' He paused. 'Believe me, it's not over.'

And it wasn't over.

That night, Cutter returned to his office on campus. He sat at his huge, untidy desk, staring into space. Then his gaze drifted to the portrait of himself and Helen. They both looked so happy. He stared at it for a moment before snatching it up and laying it face down on the desk.

Consumed by guilt, the professor worked late, marking papers written by students whose research seemed to be based on *Jurassic Park* . . .

He woke with a start, realizing at once that something had changed.

The photograph was now the right way up. And resting on top of it was a perfect fossil of an ammonite – extinct for seventy million years. Carefully, Cutter picked up the coiled shell, then dropped it in surprise as a slimy tentacle emerged from inside. Seconds later, he heard the sound of running footsteps. A door slammed. Whoever had left the ammonite was still here!

Immediately, he was on his feet, racing through the empty lab, down darkened corridors and finally out of the main entrance.

He was just in time to see the intruder pause on the edge of the campus. An unknown instinct made him stop, a sick feeling of anticipation washing over him. It was as if he already knew what he would see, even though his rational mind rejected the possibility.

The figure – it was a woman – walked into the pool of light beneath a street lamp and Cutter whispered her name under his breath.

'Helen . . .'

She smiled.

And then she stepped into the darkness.

CHAPTER 13

By the next morning, Nick Cutter's office was even messier than usual. Cabinet doors hung open, discarded files lay everywhere and in the midst of everything sat the professor, frantically leafing through handfuls of yellowing paper. He had the look of a man who hadn't slept.

Stephen was hunched over the ancient computer that was squirrelled away in the corner of the office. He frowned at the tiny screen. 'There's ten years of Helen's work here,' he groaned, tapping the keyboard to restore yet another deleted file.

'Keep looking,' mumbled Cutter.

'You've read every word she ever wrote,' protested Stephen. 'We've been through all this dozens of times before.'

'We didn't know about the anomaly then,' said the professor. 'There might be references in Helen's work that we overlooked.'

Stephen sighed. 'If she knew about it, she'd have told you.'

But Cutter didn't look so sure.

At the Home Office, Claudia was debriefing her boss. Lester – a deeply logical man – wore the vaguely shocked expression of someone who has just been told that fairies do exist. And he was not happy about it.

'So far, we've had no more creature reports,' said Claudia briskly. 'I've left Ryan in charge of mopping up. There's a lot of Internet chatter,' she continued, 'but we have natural disbelief on our side.'

'Eyewitnesses?' barked Lester.

'The teacher is in shock,' replied Claudia. 'I'm positive we can keep her away from the newspapers. And the boy is no problem.'

'Pity the monster didn't eat them,' drawled Lester. 'That would have been the neatest solution.' He clocked Claudia's appalled face. 'Joke,' he explained. 'What about Cutter?'

Claudia was suddenly on her guard. 'What about him?' she asked.

'Does the term "loose cannon" sound familiar?'

'He may be a little unconventional,' she snapped.

'But he's the closest thing we've got to an expert. Losing him now would be a mistake.'

Lester raised a quizzical eyebrow. 'You've taken to him, haven't you?' he said.

Instantly, Claudia realized that she'd let her guard down. 'I trust him, if that's what you mean,' she said quickly.

'Of course,' replied Lester calmly. 'What else?' He smiled with infuriating blandness. 'I don't like anyone to whom the adjective "maverick" might be applied. And Cutter virtually owns the copyright.' He paused and then sighed heavily. 'All right. Keep him on side for the time being.'

'I'm sure you won't regret it,' said Claudia.

'I hope not,' said her boss, his tone drier than a prehistoric desert. 'Because if I do, you'll be rubber-stamping stationery orders for the rest of your career.' He paused. 'And in case you're wondering, that wasn't a joke.'

In a university library not far away, Connor was struggling not to spill the beans. And failing miserably.

'It's more than my life's worth to say any more,' he whispered to his anorak-clad fellow geeks. 'Official

Secrets Act,' he added. And then, because he really couldn't resist, 'But I'll tell you this. I've seen a Gorgonopsid face to face. And trust me – it wasn't pretty.'

Tom, the noodle-thin geek, grinned pityingly. 'Just how stupid do you think we are, Con? Space-time anomalies, dinosaurs, package tours of the late-Permian era. Someone's been overdoing the PlayStation.'

'I can prove it!' spluttered Connor. Then he remembered the document he'd signed. 'Only I'm not allowed to.' Enraged by their sniggering, he leapt to his feet. 'One day, you'll be gutted that you didn't believe me,' he shouted, before storming out.

His friends shook their heads in bemusement.

'He's lost it,' said Duncan, the shorter and dumpier of the two.

'Totally,' replied Tom. 'What's weird is that he actually seems to believe it all himself . . .' As his voice petered out, he had a mischievous twinkle in his eye.

He began to smile.

Abby plunged her shovel deep into the pile of elephant dung and wished for the millionth time that she were working somewhere less smelly. She thought wistfully of the Reptile House. She'd give anything to be back there, doing her old job.

'They said I'd find you in here,' said a familiar voice.

Abby looked up and cringed. Stephen had arrived – gorgeous, laid-back and smelling of lemony aftershave, while she smelt of –

Stephen's nose wrinkled as he caught a whiff. 'You smell evil. What are you doing?'

'Elephant dung,' Abby said dully. 'I'm searching for parasites.'

Stephen smiled. 'I brought you something,' he said, handing her an envelope.

With a frown, she opened it and pulled out an official-looking letter. Abby's eyes widened in amazement. 'It says I've been awarded a grant,' she said. 'The Helen Cutter Educational Trust . . . It's enough to fund my research at the Reptile House for a couple of years at least. I don't understand . . .'

'Cutter liked the way you handled yourself,' said Stephen, with a shrug. 'He wants you to stick around.'

Overwhelmed with delight, Abby went to fling her arms round his neck, but Stephen stepped back smartly, his hands raised in defence. Remembering how filthy she was, Abby stood where she was and grinned instead.

'I'm sorry about your lizard,' said Stephen.

'What?'

'Rex,' he replied. 'I know how fond you were of him.'

Quickly, Abby flung a bright smile in Stephen's direction. 'Well,' she said, 'at least he's home now.' She comforted herself with the thought that she hadn't lied – not exactly. Rex was home.

CHAPTER 14

The fugitive Coelurosauravus – Abby had trawled through dusty reference books until she'd found out what he was – squatted regally inside the huge tank, watching as his new friend rushed to and fro, tending to his every need.

Buzzzzzz!

Abby jumped guiltily as the sound reverberated through the flat.

'It's Connor!' croaked the intercom.

Abby thought fast, throwing a blanket over Rex's tank before pressing the door release.

A moment later, Connor tumbled inside, staring in awe at the funky apartment and then at Abby's skimpy outfit. 'Is it me, or is it seriously hot in here?' he mumbled.

'Broken thermostat,' said Abby quickly. She wasn't about to tell Connor that she'd turned the heating up to make the surroundings more comfortable for her new flatmate. Now she just had to hope that he didn't notice the blanket-covered object in the middle of the room.

'What's that?' Connor asked.

Darn. He'd noticed it.

'Empty tank,' said Abby. 'From the zoo.' She decided to make a quick exit before he could ask any more questions. 'I'll go and get changed.'

'Read this,' said the student, shoving a piece of paper into her hand as she dashed past him and up the stairs. He'd hardly been able to contain himself when he'd discovered the rumours flying about online. He'd printed them all out, just to convince himself that his eyes weren't deceiving him.

'Where did you get this?' Abby called down to him.

'Internet,' Connor said. 'Looks like we might have another anomaly. I think we should check it out,' he added casually.

'What does Cutter say?'

'Haven't told him,' replied Connor. 'I might be wrong and I don't want him to think I'm an idiot.'

'He already thinks you're an idiot.'

Connor shrugged, not offended in the slightest. His

eyes wandered around the apartment as he waited for Abby, coming to rest again on the large object in the middle of the room. He hesitated briefly before peeping beneath the blanket, his eyes instantly lighting up with amazement.

Abby reappeared, realizing from his amused expression that Connor knew her guilty secret. 'Rex sort of . . . came back,' she mumbled.

'You kidnapped a helpless lizard!' cried Connor in mock outrage.

'I didn't want Lester's people getting hold of him again,' said Abby. 'You won't tell anyone?'

He grinned, a cunning gleam in his eyes. 'You can rely on me. We're a team, right?' Connor glanced at the piece of paper in her hand. 'So what about it? Are you in?'

Abby looked uncertain. 'Maybe we should just let someone know . . .?' she said nervously.

Sensing that her resolve was weakening, Connor really went for it. 'This is our big chance to show we can be useful,' he said. 'Come on. We're pals. And pals stick up for each other.' The student glanced meaningfully at the tank. 'Who knows, you might even find a little playmate for Rex.'

Abby knew when to give in gracefully.

She would go.

Weighed down by bulky rucksacks, they made their way through dense woods. As the daylight weakened, so Abby's unease grew.

'Maybe this wasn't a great idea,' she muttered.

Connor grinned mischievously. 'You don't want to save the world from a vicious predator?'

Abby shook her head. 'I don't think we should be doing it on our own.'

'Hold my hand if you're frightened,' offered Connor.

'How would that make me feel better?' asked Abby, quickly adding, 'Anyway, who said I was frightened?'

Connor grinned gleefully. 'I would be if I was face to face with a raptor. Just think about the teeth on those things . . . You'd be torn apart before you could blink!'

'Shut up, Connor,' snapped Abby, letting him walk on ahead. She looked round uneasily into the darkening woods, before pulling her mobile from her rucksack. Furtively, she texted a message, but as she sent it her battery died.

Great. A night in the middle of the New Forest with a monster-mad nut and the possibility that an anomaly might open up at any moment with no mobile to call for help. That was just what she needed.

CHAPTER 15

Claudia walked into Cutter's office to find him sitting cross-legged in a sea of paper. 'You didn't reply to my messages,' she began. 'So I came in person.'

'I've been busy,' said the professor.

She smiled. 'I can see that. What is it? Some kind of recycling initiative?'

'I'm going through Helen's papers,' explained Cutter. 'She always hated the daily graft of science. Big ideas were her thing. She took too many short cuts for my taste.' He looked up at her, a flicker of anguish in his eyes. 'It's my fault she disappeared.'

'Why?' Claudia asked, puzzled.

'I was supposed to go with her on that field trip,' he said sadly. 'But we had a row. Another row. We argued a lot that last year. She'd become obsessed with theories I found . . . ridiculous.'

Claudia stiffened. 'You mean she was on to the anomaly,' she said slowly.

'Not as such,' Cutter replied. 'But she was convinced that there were no conventional scientific answers to certain evolutionary puzzles.' He paused. 'Obviously, she was right.'

'No one could have guessed that,' Claudia said softly, trying to understand what torment Cutter must have gone through in the last eight years – and was still going through now.

'She did.'

'You're not to blame for her death.'

'What makes you so sure she's dead?'

'She was lost two hundred million years away in the past. What else could she be?'

It was stalemate.

Cutter stared at his inquisitor, as if on the brink of a monumental announcement – and then the moment passed. 'So, tell me the plan,' he said lightly.

'What plan?' Claudia felt disorientated at the speed the conversation had changed direction. 'What else can we do?'

'We could start by telling people the truth,' Cutter suggested.

'Let me think about that.' Claudia raised an eyebrow. 'No. Right now, this is all just a rumour mill for Internet conspiracy freaks. We can contain that. The alternatives – panic, hysteria, potential lawlessness – simply aren't viable.'

'Connor will be thrilled,' said Cutter with a wry chuckle. 'A genuine cover-up to enjoy.'

'It's not a cover-up,' Claudia said quickly. Then she stopped and wrinkled her nose thoughtfully. 'OK – it is. But it has to be done. And if you have a problem with that, you'd better say so now.'

The professor flinched at her forceful manner, but before he had time to reply, Stephen crashed into the room.

'Text from Abby,' he gasped. 'Connor thinks he's on to another anomaly . . . creature sighting, the lot. They've gone to investigate.'

'Where the hell are they?' cried Cutter, his eyes blazing with anger.

'The New Forest – she's not sure exactly where.'

Cutter whirled round to face Claudia. 'Can you trace her mobile?'

As Abby clutched Rex, a menacing growl filled the forest.

'Your wife went missing here, didn't she?' Claudia asked Cutter.

The team looked up to see the dead cow
suspended in the branches.

The needle on the compass was spinning around like crazy.

The mighty predator stalked through the school,
looking for its prey.

'I'm going through the anomaly,' Cutter told Lester.

Abby couldn't help but worry as the scientists examined Rex.

The massive Gorgonopsid chased Stephen
down the school corridor.

The professor gazed around the bleak Permian landscape.

Vast herds of prehistoric creatures
were dotted about the hills.

Cutter was overwhelmed with relief. The skeleton wasn't Helen.

Something was down in the long-abandoned tube station.

The bunker came alive with a seething mass of giant spiders.

The giant centipede prepared to strike.

CHAPTER 16

Connor leant against a tree, waiting for Abby to emerge from her tent. Tonight was the night. Abby would finally realize how wonderfully clever and lovable he was – and together they would discover the anomaly, step through it and find a dinosaur or two. And true love, obviously.

Excellent.

His mobile rang, ruining the moment utterly. Connor saw Stephen's name appear on the tiny screen and immediately switched the phone to silent. The lab technician wasn't even here and he was still getting in the way of a beautiful friendship.

'My tent's only big enough for one,' Abby said, clambering out of it. 'You should have brought your own.'

'I like sleeping out,' said Connor, despite the disappointment sweeping over him. 'I did the Duke of Edinburgh Award, you know. For a morning.' He grinned ruefully. 'Then I hurt my ankle.'

Abby smiled, taking the plastic cup of tea he offered her. She sipped it gratefully, shivering a little with cold. Then, her cheeks suddenly pink, she turned quickly to Connor. 'Can I ask you a personal question?' she said.

Connor felt a surge of hope. This was it – the moment he'd waited for. 'Go ahead,' he said. 'Anything.'

'Is Stephen seeing anyone?' she asked.

'Stephen?' Connor's spirits plummeted.

'Has he said anything about me?' Abby continued.

Connor shrugged. 'Not that I remember,' he said sullenly. Noticing Abby's disappointed expression, he suddenly saw an opportunity to make her feel as bad as he did. 'Actually . . . I've never seen him with a woman. He might not like them.'

Abby absorbed this unwanted information in silence, before hurling the rest of her tea across the forest floor. She stomped over to her tent and ducked inside, zipping it up firmly.

'I'll keep first watch then, shall I . . .?' Connor said. He contemplated the tatty sleeping bag beside him and sighed.

*

'Wake up!'

Confused and disorientated, Connor jolted awake to find Abby shaking him. He was about to protest when he heard a low animal growl. An uneasy silence followed. Then – crash! – a heavy tread smashed through the undergrowth just metres away.

Abby caught a glimpse of a reptilian head silhouetted against the trees. 'Oh my . . .' she breathed, as a spine-chilling growl echoed through the forest.

Connor looked around in panic, before signalling to Abby to make a break for it. At the same moment, the creature burst from the trees, its hideous, snarling features clearer in the moonlight. The terrified student grabbed a pathetic-looking stick and turned to confront the monster –

Clunk! It promptly fell over.

The student grabbed for his torch and shone it on the dinosaur, which lay unmoving on the forest floor. Its jaws hung wide open and its eyes were still. Was it dead? If so, what had killed it? Quickly, Connor swept the torch's beam along the length of its body, seeing at once that they were the victims of an elaborate hoax. The creature was not made of flesh and blood, but of papier-mâché and latex. It sat atop an old pram. Behind it, doubled up with laughter, stood Connor's geek friends from university. They carried a digital recorder, which was emitting lifelike roars and crashes.

'Careful!' called Tom. 'It bites!'

Duncan howled with glee.

But before Connor could react, headlights swept through the woods and a car pulled up. A police officer got out and stared at the strange scene, looking totally bemused by what he saw. Swiftly, Tom and Duncan disappeared into the safety of the forest, just as Cutter and Stephen arrived.

Connor gulped. He was in trouble. Big trouble.

Once the police officer was satisfied that this was no more than a student prank, he left. Nick Cutter walked over to Connor and Abby. He looked so angry that they were more afraid than when they'd been confronted by the cardboard beast.

'I know what you're going to say,' Connor began.

'Sorry,' added Abby, shamefaced.

'You're lucky the police aren't going to prosecute you for trespassing,' snapped Cutter. Furiously, he turned to Connor. 'Suppose it really had been a predator. What were you going to do? Tame it? You knew exactly what was at stake, but you just couldn't keep your mouth shut.'

Connor swallowed hard, realizing that he had to come clean. 'It's just so big,' he admitted. 'I had to share it with someone . . .' He hung his head. 'I'm sorry. I blew it.'

The professor's next words hit him like a sledgehammer blow. 'Forget the anomaly,' he said. 'It never happened. Go back to college and get on with your work. I'll find you another supervisor.'

'I'm just as much to blame as he is,' Abby said quickly.

'Just as stupid, maybe,' said Cutter. 'But you didn't tell anyone and you still have skills I can use. You stay.'

Abby felt a terrible mixture of relief and guilt. However mean Connor had been about Stephen, he certainly didn't deserve this.

As he stood forlornly in the New Forest, Connor had no way of knowing that he was right. There was another anomaly. But it wasn't anywhere near the New Forest. And it had nothing to do with dinosaurs – fake or otherwise. Deep underneath the city of London, trouble was brewing . . .

CHAPTER 17

'This kind of thing doesn't normally interest the government,' said Dr Lewis, looking at the unconscious man in the hospital bed. She knew the drill. Any sort of crime and the police were involved. This time, it was different. She was being treated to a visit from a Home Office official and a university professor. Why did this poor victim warrant such attention?

Claudia answered briskly. 'We like to keep an eye on violent crime, especially where there are unusual circumstances.' She and Cutter regarded the patient, who was hooked up to an array of life-support machines. Violent spasms shook his body, but the only sign of injury was the bandage wrapped round his neck.

'They found him in the Underground early this morning,' explained the doctor. 'He's a pest controller. Judging from the size of his wound, he'd been attacked with a knife or an axe.' She paused. 'But it makes no sense . . . It's not the wound that's killing him. It's the poison. His system is drowning in it.'

Claudia went pale. 'You're suggesting that someone took an axe to him and then injected poison into the wound?'

'Venom, to be precise,' said Dr Lewis. 'We're running every test we can think of, but the truth is that we just don't know what we're dealing with.'

'Did he say anything before he lost consciousness?' Claudia went on.

The doctor's reply was offhand. 'He was babbling about monsters – not very helpful.'

Cutter and Claudia shared an uneasy look, then watched as Dr Lewis peeled back the patient's dressing to reveal an ugly gash in his neck.

The professor spoke up. 'It's a single puncture, but it wasn't made by a knife,' he said. 'It's more like a bite.'

This changed everything.

Lester was both furious and dismayed. He was furious because Claudia's demand was nothing short of outrageous. And he was dismayed because another unbelievable case had arrived to disturb his inner calm – and the ink had barely dried on the first one.

'I can't close the Underground on a wild hunch,' he protested.

Cutter's reply was curt. 'Something down there injected a fatal dose of venom into his bloodstream,' he said.

'And how do you suggest I explain this to the mayor?' Lester spluttered. 'Excuse me, sir. Would you mind terribly throwing the whole Underground into chaos because we think there might be a fare-dodging creepy-crawly loose somewhere?'

'We're not talking about shutting down the system,' Claudia said hurriedly. 'Just the area where the attack took place. There's a whole network of disused tunnels down there.'

Lester looked at her bitterly, not even bothering to hide his contempt. Then, finally, he nodded his consent.

The SAS were on the case. Ryan and his team hurtled through the streets of London in unmarked cars, skidding to a halt outside Aldwych tube station. Within minutes, the road was sealed off and a stream of military personnel was pouring down the escalators into the depths of the Underground system. The fluorescent bibs they wore signalled to curious onlookers that they were staff. And no one suspected that the clinking holdalls they carried were crammed with anything other than maintenance equipment. After all, Lester had made it very clear that if a single member of the public were to suspect what was going on, the whole team would be for the high jump.

A dusty staircase led them into the depths of the system and away from the crowds. Once out of sight, the team dumped their bibs and clamped on night-vision goggles. The holdalls were unzipped to reveal a stash of hi-tech rifles.

Ryan consulted a diagram and gave a brief nod in the direction of a locked door at the foot of the stairs. A quick snip later, the bolt-cutter had dispatched the padlock as if it were made of butter. Behind the door was a dusty, long-forgotten corridor that stretched back into inky darkness. Pausing only to clamp on their goggles, Ryan and his team strode forward.

'I should be down there with them,' Cutter mumbled, staring at the tarmac as if imagining the events taking place far below them.

He, Claudia, Stephen and Abby were gathered at the temporary command centre that had sprung up outside the long-abandoned tube station. To the general public, it might look like an ordinary van, but inside was enough computer equipment to hack into the Bank of England.

'Special Forces go in first,' said Claudia patiently. 'You didn't think Lester was going to let you have it all your own way?' She gave him a sideways glance. 'Anyway, he knows how valuable you are to us. He's trying to keep you safe.'

The professor grinned. 'Is that true?' he asked.

'No,' she replied, smiling back at him. 'But I thought it might make you feel better.'

The wartime bunker was crammed with half a century of junk. Ancient rubbish littered the floor – piles of wood, dust-covered bottles of turpentine and stacks of yellow, curling Underground posters. No one had been here for a very long time.

No one.

But *something* had been here much more recently.

Ryan gazed around the room, trying to ignore a feeling of growing unease. Then out of the corner of his eye he thought he saw something – a scuttling movement that made him think of an insect. But it couldn't have been. Insects weren't that big.

The sense of dread threatened to overwhelm him. Then instinct made him turn sharply to look at one of his men standing just behind. Through the night-vision goggles, it seemed that his outline was quivering. No . . . It was worse than that. Something was climbing up the man's back, reaching a long, hairy limb over his shoulder –

Thwack!

Ryan swung the butt of his rifle at the huge mutant spider – measuring nearly a metre across – and it fell to the ground, quickly running into a dark corner. The soldier gave him a grateful nod.

Then, just when it seemed as if the danger was over, chunky balls of fur began to fall from above. Ryan's eyes flicked upwards and what he saw made his skin crawl. The ceiling was alive with movement. Ever since they had entered the bunker, the seething mass of giant spiders had been above them. And now the creatures were attacking.

'Argh!' shouted one of the soldiers as he was bitten.

In slow motion, another soldier raised his rifle to eye level and aimed at the enormous spider balanced precariously on top of a packing crate.

'Hold your fire!' commanded Ryan.

Too late.

The shot rang out, missing its target and ricocheting around the room at high velocity. The bullet flared like a torch, leaving a blindingly bright trail behind it.

Ryan watched in horror as more shots were fired.

His men were in danger. Any second now, one of them would catch a stray bullet. There was only one thing to do.

'Withdraw!' he ordered.

The SAS were in a bad way. Pale, sweaty and nauseous, they looked more like plague victims than an elite fighting force. Paramedics whisked away the injured soldier, blood flowing from his wound. Cutter and his team crowded around Ryan to hear his story.

'They were like spiders . . . but with pincers . . . not fangs,' the soldier gasped, his words punctuated by violent coughing and retching. 'Some of them were over a metre long . . . horrible little –'

Cutter interrupted him with a frown. 'Tell me exactly how you feel,' he said.

'Sick,' replied Ryan. 'Can't stop coughing. And my ears are ringing.'

'Any blurred vision?'

He nodded. 'There was something else too. The gunshots – they were too bright, like fireworks.'

This was just the clue that Stephen needed. 'Classic signs of excess oxygen in the atmosphere,' he said.

Cutter nodded. Seeing that Claudia looked puzzled, he clarified the situation. 'Richer, more heavily oxygenated air must be seeping in through another anomaly. We're not talking the Permian period any longer. This is much earlier, maybe the Carboniferous. About three hundred million years ago.' A determined expression appeared on his craggy face. 'We need to find out exactly what these creatures are. I have to see for myself.'

'I'm ready . . .' began Ryan, standing up. But he stumbled dizzily.

'You're staying here,' said Claudia, supporting him.

But Cutter was growing impatient. He needed to get down there and fast. 'Give me a chance to do my job,' he said.

Claudia nodded. She knew there was no other choice.

It didn't take long for Cutter to get kitted out. Abby and Stephen would be going too – they looked nervous, but excited. All three wore protective clothing, gloves and heavy boots.

'We'll need torches,' Cutter told Ryan. 'The most powerful you can find.'

'Take the night-vision goggles,' suggested the soldier.

Cutter shook his head. 'Vision isn't the issue.'

Wearing a puzzled frown, Ryan hurried away to be replaced by Claudia, who had just finished speaking on her mobile. She didn't look happy.

'The pest controller died a few minutes ago,' she said. 'They're running more tests on our casualty now.' Then Claudia spotted Abby, registering her heavy-duty overalls. 'What's she doing?' she demanded crossly.

'Abby's had more practical experience with animals than the rest of us put together,' said Cutter.

'I don't care if she's Doctor Dolittle,' snapped Claudia. 'It's too risky.'

'I can help,' said Abby, smiling earnestly. 'I've just finished a study in insect behaviour.'

The woman from the Home Office appeared unconvinced, but nevertheless gave her grudging consent. As she hurried away, Stephen smiled knowingly at Abby.

'Is that true?'

'Kind of,' replied Abby. 'If parasites count.' The bright grin didn't hide her nervousness and she shrugged. 'To tell you the truth, spiders aren't really my thing.'

Stephen gave her a wry smile. 'Technically, these are probably scorpions.'

Abby nodded thoughtfully. 'Like spiders, only three feet long. I feel better already.'

'Stay near me,' Cutter's assistant joked. 'I need protecting.'

Their eyes met, both of them suddenly very aware that something was going on here. But the spell was broken by Claudia's return.

'Keep in touch at all times,' she said, thrusting a radio receiver into Cutter's gloved hand. And it wasn't a request. It was an order.

CHAPTER 19

Beams of torchlight sliced through the darkness as they made their way through the bunker, the blinding brightness sending spiders scattering left and right. The team of three gazed around, taking in the cluttered surroundings, the abandoned equipment and – above all – the atmosphere of foreboding.

Stephen stifled a grunt of disgust as a horribly furry insect dropped from the ceiling in his path. He kicked out at it.

Meanwhile, Cutter was examining a door at the far end of the bunker. 'Where does that lead?' he asked.

Stephen shrugged. 'Dead end . . .'

'Cutter!' Her face ghostly in the low light, Abby appeared mesmerized, until the others realized that the dusty air before her was moving. A small patch – no bigger than a chessboard – was more opaque than the rest. And this was where the spiders were heading. One by one, they scampered towards it, their many feet scratching on the concrete floor.

Then they vanished into thin air.

'What's happening to us?' breathed Cutter as the three of them watched the anomaly, utterly transfixed.

Abby's torch slid from her fingers, clattering noisily on to the floor. Jerked out of her reverie, she bent to retrieve it and caught a glimpse of a truly monstrous creature, towering above her. As the light hit it, the enormous thing let out a long, angry hiss, then leapt forward, its deadly mouth wide open, with saliva dripping from razor-sharp pincers.

Screaming with terror, Abby dived out of the way. And the hideous creature retracted its massive body and vanished behind a pile of boxes, as quickly as it had appeared. Stephen rushed to Abby's side. They could hear it creeping through the shadows, but despite swinging their torches around they failed to catch more than the briefest glimpse of the monster. Then without warning, it lunged at them again, sending Abby and Stephen sprawling across the room.

Cutter was next on the monster's hit list. But he was ready, hurling himself out of the reach of the deadly pincers at the last minute. He spoke desperately into the radio from his hiding place behind a pile of wood.

'There's another creature in here. We're coming out!'

Together, Stephen and Abby made for the exit, closely followed by the huge creature. In a last-ditch attempt to distract it, Stephen flung a bottle he found lying on the floor against the wall. As it smashed, the monster shied away from the noise, giving them a chance to get out.

'Cutter!' cried Stephen, as the beast changed direction and blocked the professor's escape route.

'I'm OK!' shouted Cutter. 'Go! I'm right behind you!'

Reluctantly, Stephen went, dragging Abby with him.

But Cutter was trapped. Behind him was a wall and in front of him was the biggest centipede he'd ever clapped eyes on. As he raised his arm to brush one of the smaller spiders – only the size of an octopus – from his arm, the radio slid from his grasp. Instantly, the magnetic pull of the quivering anomaly sucked it across the room – and into another dimension. Things weren't going well.

Meanwhile, the centipede was moving closer, ever closer. The professor watched it approach, leaving it as late as he dared to make his move. Then, when he could feel the monster's rancid breath on his forehead, he hurled the torch into its face. Stunned by the attack, it retreated for a split second. This was all the time Cutter needed to leap through the other door – and into a dead-end tunnel.

He braced himself against the door, breathing heavily, sweat trickling down his face. Thump! The door shuddered as the creature flung its weight against it – but it held.

Cutter ripped off his mask and threw it to one side. By the dim light of the tiny torch on his key ring, he scanned his surroundings. He couldn't see anything clearly, although he seemed to be in some sort of tunnel. A second later, he heard the shuffling of footsteps.

'Who's there?' he called, feeling uneasy. He saw a faint outline just metres away and raised his torch – by its feeble light, he saw a ghostly shape flitting away. It was a woman's shape . . .

'Helen?' he said. 'Helen!'

CHAPTER 20

The street was hectic with activity.

In a quiet corner, Abby, Stephen and Claudia pored over a map of the Underground.

'All I'm getting is interference!' snapped Claudia, impatiently throwing her radio receiver away. She frowned at the map. 'There's no other way out. The tunnel was blocked up thirty years ago.'

'Then why isn't he back yet?' said Abby.

Stephen looked stricken with guilt. 'I should never have left him,' he said. 'He must be trapped. I'm going back in.'

Claudia shook her head. 'No one's going anywhere until we know what we're dealing with.'

'He could be injured –' protested Stephen.

The woman from the Home Office interrupted him. 'I don't want to leave him down there any more than you do. But I'm not losing anyone else on a wild goose chase. We don't even know for sure where he is.'

Stephen couldn't argue with this.

'Did he say what kind of creature it was?' Claudia continued.

He shook his head. 'Some kind of centipede . . .'

'But huge,' added Abby. 'Five metres, at least.'

'I need more,' said Claudia. 'Preferred habitat, behaviour patterns, strengths and weaknesses . . .'

'We don't know,' replied Abby helplessly. 'No one does.'

For the first time in hours, Stephen's face creased into a wide smile. 'Connor might.'

As soon as Claudia hurried away to trace Connor, Stephen made his move.

'I'm not leaving Cutter in there a minute longer than I have to,' he whispered urgently to Abby.

'You can't go back down without backup,' she replied, fear showing in her eyes.

'Watch me.'

For a second, it seemed as if Abby might try to stop Stephen. But instead, she simply hugged him tightly.

Then – pausing only to grab a discarded radio receiver – he ran back into the ancient Underground system, almost tumbling down the dusty staircase in his hurry to reach his boss.

Suddenly realizing that he carried no weapon, he wrenched open the doors he passed, eventually finding a storeroom filled with cleaning supplies. A plastic container with a metal nozzle was the best he could find. Shrugging, he took it with him.

It didn't take long to reach the room where he'd last seen the professor. Now it was eerily still.

'Cutter?' whispered Stephen.

He moved inside cautiously, stopping as he spotted the turpentine. Quickly, he emptied a couple of bottles into his container, all the time checking carefully for any sign of movement. Then he ventured further into the room, expecting to hear or see the beast with every step he took. But all was quiet, although the door at the far end of the room was now dented and twisted. Had the monster gone?

He twisted the handle and gently pushed the battered door open, his torchlight showing a corridor stretching away into darkness. Hearing a noise behind him, he spun round –

Wham!

With a powerful blow, the centipede smashed into the torch, knocking it from his grasp. Stephen fought back at once, aiming the spray bottle at the creature and squirting turpentine into its hideous face. It shied away violently, an unearthly rattling emerging from its body as it vanished behind a heap of boxes. Shocked by the creature's attack, Stephen loosened his grip on the bottle of turpentine.

Whoosh!

He'd forgotten about the anomaly. Its magnetic pull had attracted the metal nozzle and yanked the whole spray bottle towards the patch of quivering, sparkling air. As if sensing that Stephen was unarmed, the centipede moved with incredible speed, clamping on tightly with its many legs, while sinking its pincers into his shoulder. Despite the excruciating pain, Stephen fought to escape the deadly embrace, lashing out repeatedly until finally it released him and dropped to the floor, slithering away into the darkness.

Stephen grasped his injured shoulder – it felt wet and sticky. Blood. Suddenly, a wave of nausea washed over him and his legs gave way. He tried to haul himself up, but his arms had no strength either.

'Stephen? Are you OK?'

Abby's voice crackled through the radio receiver. But it was hopelessly out of reach of his scrabbling fingers. Within seconds, they too ceased to function as the creeping paralysis overcame his entire body. Stephen struggled to keep panic at bay.

He sensed rather than saw the anomaly move. Footsteps sounded. And hope flared in Stephen – someone had come to rescue him!

'Over here!' he croaked.

No reply.

'Why don't you say something?' he pleaded, unable to look round.

Finally, the silent figure walked into Stephen's line of vision. His eyes widened in amazement and he whispered a single, incredulous word through cracked and drying lips.

'Helen?'

When Cutter made his way back along the tunnel, he saw that the door was now open. He paused at the entrance to the bunker, scanning the darkened room for any sign of the centipede. Nothing. Cautiously, he walked forward and spotted Stephen's torch lying on the floor, its beam pointing towards the softly glittering anomaly. He heard a groan and spun round to see Stephen propped up against a pile of old boxes, his body shaking.

Cutter rushed over to him. 'What happened?' he gasped.

'Argument with a big bug,' murmured Stephen, with a faint smile. 'Bug won.'

Swiftly, Cutter pulled back the bloodsoaked cloth of his shirt to reveal a gaping wound. 'Let's get you out of here,' he said.

But the younger man had something to tell him first. 'Helen's alive,' he slurred. 'She was here. She gave me a message . . . She's waiting on the other side of the anomaly. She said that if you want to know the truth, you'll have to come to find her.'

Not even the sobering news that Cutter and Stephen were missing underground could dampen Connor's enthusiasm. He'd been given a second chance. And he wasn't going to mess it up this time.

'Carboniferous . . . probably an Arthropleurid . . .' He nodded, absorbing the information he'd been given while simultaneously whizzing through his database. 'Centipede on steroids, basically,' he announced. 'More or less blind, good sense of smell and touch . . . prefers the dark, obviously . . . big and scary-looking, but actually quite timid. The kind of bug that sticks to the kitchen at parties.'

Claudia peered over his shoulder at the laptop screen. 'This one must have a personality disorder,' she said. 'How dangerous is it?'

'According to the textbooks,' Connor replied importantly, 'it would have eaten dead wood and leaves.'

'So it's not poisonous?'

'No way.'

At that moment, there was a sudden flurry of activity by the tube station as Cutter emerged, dragging Stephen with him.

'He's been bitten by the Arthropleurid,' the professor said hurriedly. 'Identical wound and same symptoms as the pest controller. We have to do something before the poison destroys his central nervous system.'

Connor stared at him, aghast. 'Poison?'

'The spiders are off the hook,' replied Cutter. 'It's the centipede that's the killer.'

Claudia gave Connor a scathing look. 'How did we ever manage without you?' she said, her words laced with sarcasm.

'I was only speculating . . .' mumbled Connor, crestfallen.

But no one was paying him any attention now. All eyes were on Stephen, who lay on a stretcher, with anxious paramedics in attendance. 'Tell them,' he muttered suddenly. 'Tell them about Helen.'

Claudia looked at Cutter in surprise, but he feigned ignorance. 'What's he talking about?' she demanded.

'I . . . don't know,' lied Cutter. 'He must be hallucinating.'

'He seems quite lucid to me,' said Claudia, giving the professor a searching look.

Cutter ignored her, turning his attention to Stephen instead. The paramedics had completed their checks and had opened the waiting ambulance's doors, ready to whisk him inside.

Abby rushed over to grab the patient's hand.

'You know, you're really beautiful,' Stephen sighed.

She grinned, even though she felt like crying. 'You're delirious,' she replied.

'Have dinner with me.'

'We'll talk about it when you're better.'

'Can't wait that long.'

Abby bent close and whispered in his ear. 'Yes, I will.'

'Result,' murmured Stephen, his eyelids closing as the paramedics wheeled him inside the ambulance. 'Amazing how much easier this stuff is when you're dying.'

Abby clambered into the vehicle with him. 'You're not dying,' she insisted, as the tears finally threatened to fall.

But they both knew that he was.

'Who did this to him?' demanded Dr Lewis.

'It's . . . hard to explain,' mumbled Abby. A giant centipede? Yeah, right. Like anyone would believe that.

'If we don't find out exactly what bit him,' the doctor said ominously, 'he'll die.'

Abby swallowed hard. 'It was a centipede.' Without waiting for the doctor to disagree, she added fiercely, 'Look, we can stand here arguing about how impossible that is, or you can just take my word for it. Please?'

There was a moment's silence. When the doctor's reply came, it was calm and rational. 'There are no obvious treatments,' she said. 'People just don't die of centipede bites. But if we can get hold of a good sample of the venom, we might be able to find an antivenin that matches it.'

'Will that make him better?' asked Abby anxiously. She'd only known him for a few days, but suddenly it was very important that Stephen survived.

'Antivenins are a last resort, toxic in their own right,' explained Dr Lewis. 'The survival rate can be as low as 50 per cent. But without it, his chances are nil.'

Abby stared wild-eyed at the doctor. 'Just keep him alive,' she said. 'Please.'

Abby dodged her way in and out of London's busy traffic to arrive back at the tube station just minutes later. Cutter, Claudia and a barely repentant Connor listened to her breathless update with worried expressions.

'Can't they run more tests?' asked Claudia. 'Find a match for the venom somehow?'

'It would take too long,' replied Abby quickly. 'Stephen's dying right now.'

Cutter had been thinking deeply and now he spoke up. 'There's only one way to short cut the process. We have to collect a pure sample of venom from the creature that bit him.'

'How the hell do we do that?' asked Claudia. 'Ask it to fill a specimen jar?'

'In a way . . .' Cutter said mysteriously.

Connor twigged what he meant at once. 'Oh, come on . . .' he said.

'It's the only option,' said the professor.

Claudia's confused gaze switched back and forth between the professor and his student. Were they deliberately trying to confuse her? 'What is?' she asked. 'Someone talk to me!'

But Cutter ignored her, grabbed a radio and spoke into that instead. 'Ryan?' he barked. 'Ryan, are you there?'

CHAPTER 22

'Ryan?' said the crackly voice. 'Ryan, are you there?'

The soldier watched the last of the mutant spiders scuttle away into the anomaly and unhooked the radio from his belt. 'The first zone's clear,' he said. Using brushes, nets and enough floodlights to illuminate Wembley Stadium, they'd obliterated all evidence of the ghastly infestation from the underground corridor. Now for the next stage of their mission. 'We're moving into the bunker,' he said.

'Have you seen the centipede?' asked Cutter.

'No trace of it yet.'

The reply was unambiguous. 'On no account let it return through the anomaly,' said Cutter. 'Repeat, do not let it go.'

Cutter tucked the radio receiver in his pocket. 'Find me something to do the job!' he shouted to Connor.

Obediently, Connor rushed away.

'What are you going to do?' asked Claudia in utter bewilderment.

Cutter grinned. 'Invite a very angry centipede to bite me.'

In the wartime bunker, the dark, forbidding shadows were now replaced by bright, welcoming light. Ryan and his team were waiting by the flickering anomaly when Cutter and the others arrived.

'The corridor's clear,' said the soldier. 'And the centipede hasn't gone through the anomaly on my watch. There's nowhere else for it to go. Either it was in here or it's still out there.' He pointed to the battered door.

With a curt nod, Cutter strode across the bunker, his boots echoing on the concrete floor. Taking out a powerful torch, he raised it high, then flung the door open and led the charge into the tunnel, the SAS pouring in after him.

It was empty.

Cutter turned back to stare at Claudia, his eyes filled with torment. 'It's gone back,' he said. 'We've lost it.'

This was bad news. The hopeful atmosphere was

replaced by a sense of gloom. Without the Arthropleura and its venom, Stephen was doomed.

'If Stephen hadn't come back for me, he wouldn't have been hurt,' Cutter groaned, staring into the black heart of the anomaly.

Claudia tried in vain to make him feel better. 'It wasn't your fault,' she said softly, a comforting hand on his shoulder.

The sound of running footsteps announced a new arrival and Connor came hurtling into the bunker, his eyes blazing with triumph. Immediately, he started manically pushing boxes out of the way, trying to get at the walls.

'Help me!' he cried to the stunned onlookers. When no one moved, he tried again. 'I'd forgotten! Arthropleurids were supposed to be burrowers. Look for a hole, anywhere the floor's rotted away.'

It took a split second for the words to sink in, then everyone joined him, shifting boxes and assorted rubbish with the same ferocious energy. At first, it seemed that they were getting nowhere, but suddenly Connor whooped with delight.

'Yes!' he crowed. 'I was right – it's still here!'

Claudia couldn't help smiling at his excitement.

When the student looked at her for approval, she nodded at once. 'Good work,' she said.

In a flash, Cutter was sprawled commando-style on the floor, shining his torch into the hole. 'How long could the tunnel be?' he asked.

'For a creature that size?' Connor thought for a moment. 'Fifty feet, maybe?'

'Fine,' said Cutter. 'I'm going in.'

'That's crazy . . .' gasped Claudia.

Cutter shrugged, as if he had no choice. 'There's no better way of finding out where it's gone,' he said.

'I'm coming too,' said Connor quickly, eager to make amends for his stupid behaviour earlier.

The professor nodded. Then he calmly helped himself to three bottles of turpentine from the pile nearby, throwing one to Ryan and another to Connor. The third he upended over himself. 'Put that on your clothes,' he told the others. 'Centipedes hate it.'

CHAPTER 23

The narrow passage was damp, dark and very cold. Whenever they brushed against the sides, they crumbled, coating the intrepid monster hunters with wet soil. As they crawled onwards, the bones of previous victims crunched beneath their knees. For Connor, who really didn't like small spaces, the end couldn't come soon enough and he breathed a huge sigh of relief as they emerged into a cavernous space.

They were in an electricity substation, part of the complex workings of the Underground system. A metal staircase led up to high walkways, several metres above them. No other tunnels led from the room, which could mean only one thing . . . The centipede was here.

Ryan shone his torch up the stairs. 'Could it really have climbed up there?' he said wonderingly.

'Let's find out,' said Cutter, heading for the

staircase. Ryan tried to muscle in and lead the way, but the professor shook his head. 'It has to be me it gets to first,' he said firmly.

Reluctantly, the soldier nodded and let him go first.

Connor hung back. He was in no hurry to climb the stairs. 'Claustrophobia and vertigo on the same day,' he groaned, looking up at the flimsy metal structure. 'Fabulous.'

Slowly, carefully, his eyes flicking to and fro for any glimpse of the monstrous creature, Cutter began his ascent. Ryan and Connor followed. The air was thick with dust and the only sound was that of their footsteps echoing on the metal steps. Above all, there was the nerve-jangling fear that the Arthropleura might dart out from the shadows at any moment. Every shadowy gap in the wall looked sinister . . .

They emerged on to a high platform to be greeted by an ominous yellow sign: DANGER OF DEATH.

Connor gulped. He didn't need reminding.

'We're in an electricity substation on the surface,' Ryan barked into his radio. 'Seal all exits immediately. Repeat, seal all possible exits.'

From up here, Cutter had a bird's-eye view of the enormous room. Thick cables snaked from the floor up the walls and into ceramic fuse boxes, while a grey metal cube as big as a family car dominated everything. He knew that this was the transformer – a device that transferred electrical energy from one circuit to another. Mounted on the wall was a metal grid housing the fuse box. More signs warning of the massive voltages travelling through this room were displayed all around.

Connor eyed the warning signs nervously, tripping over an upturned metal stool as he made his way round the transformer box. He picked up the stool, brandishing it in front of him like a lion tamer's chair. Meanwhile, Ryan cocked his rifle.

They went forward, Cutter still leading the way. The first corner was clear, then the next. Finally, there was only one corner of the platform left to check. And that's where the Arthropleura was waiting for them. The monster lay curled round the base of the huge transformer. Lazily, it lifted its head, a ripple spreading through its vast, segmented body. Connor paled, dropping the metal stool, which fell to the floor with a resounding clang.

The noise sent a tremor through the creature. With lightning speed, it darted forward, hurtling straight towards Cutter. Not even attempting to avoid the attack, the professor stood his ground, flinging up an arm at the last second in what appeared to be a futile gesture of self-defence.

With an audible crunch, the centipede sank its pincers into Cutter's forearm, the force of the assault knocking him to the floor, where he writhed helplessly under the sheer weight of the huge creature. Connor leapt forward and battered the Arthropleura with the stool, forcing it to relinquish its grasp on the professor's arm. The animal retreated to a corner.

Nursing his arm, Cutter ripped aside the damaged material of the protective jacket to reveal, strapped to his wrist, a clear plastic container filled with cloudy liquid. The huge pincers had punctured the plastic – leaving the deadly venom to collect inside.

Connor grinned – his plan had worked!

There was no time to gloat. The monster was readying itself for another attack. Ryan raised his rifle, but registered the yellow warning signs and thought better of shooting in such a dangerous environment.

But Cutter was the target, not Ryan. The centipede loomed over him, poised to strike, when Connor came to the rescue. He dashed forward, keeping the creature at bay with the metal stool. The Arthropleura opened its mighty jaws wide, preparing to retaliate – and that was just the opportunity Connor needed. He rammed the stool between the creature's jaws.

It stuck fast.

And that was when the giant centipede's luck really ran out. As it slithered past the fuse box, there was a moment of contact – metal stool and metal fuse plate touched. At once, there was a fizzing, popping sound and an explosion of sparks as 750,000 volts coursed through the fuse plate . . . along the chair leg . . . and into the creature's mouth.

Zap!

The centipede was flung into the air as a massive bolt of electricity surged through it. The creature from the far side of the anomaly was history. Or rather, it was charcoal.

Connor and Ryan stared aghast at the smoking remains of the Arthropleura, covering their noses against the terrible smell. But Cutter didn't have time to linger. Clutching his precious container of venom, he began his long scramble back up the tunnel.

CHAPTER 24

'How are you feeling?' asked Claudia.

Stephen groaned. 'Like I gargled with sand and slept inside a tumble drier.' He lay back against the cool cotton of the hospital pillowcases and glanced at the drip that now hung empty beside his bed. Thanks to Cutter, the antivenin had done its job, dragging him back from the brink of death. He grinned up at Abby, who was watching over him protectively.

Claudia smiled, then studied the patient thoughtfully. 'So, tell me about Helen,' she said.

'What about her?' asked Stephen, a frown creasing his pale forehead.

'You saw her.'

'I saw her? When?'

'In the tunnel,' Claudia spoke clearly and slowly, as if Stephen were still drugged up. 'That's what you said.'

He shrugged. 'I must have been off my head. To tell

the truth, I don't remember anything. I was probably just hallucinating.'

'Probably.' Claudia smiled briefly and nodded a goodbye before leaving the room.

Stephen looked at Abby. 'What was that all about?'

She hesitated before replying. 'You really can't remember anything after you were bitten? None of the things you said in the ambulance?'

'Why?' he said, his expression blank. 'What did I say?'

'Oh, just . . . stuff,' murmured Abby. 'I thought some of it might have stuck . . .'

Stephen shook his head. 'No. Was it important?'

Abby shrugged casually to hide her disappointment. 'Not really,' she said. If Stephen couldn't remember their conversation after his accident, she certainly wasn't going to remind him. She didn't want to look a fool.

'Thanks for looking after me,' Stephen said, smiling gratefully. 'You're a mate.'

A mate.

It was all Abby could do to smile back.

The wartime bunker was still buzzing with activity. Soldiers and scientists vied with each other for elbow space, every person intent on completing their own vital task before the bunker was sealed up for good.

Cutter ignored them all. There was only one thing in that underground room that held his interest – the anomaly. He stood gazing at it, a weary tension in his face, gradually becoming aware that someone was standing beside him.

'I just wanted to check . . .' Connor ventured hesitantly. 'Am I back in?'

The professor sighed. 'Can we keep you out?'

Connor tried again. 'I only want to help.'

'You did a good job,' admitted Cutter.

The student grinned proudly. 'All my life I've wanted to be in a crime-busting gang,' he gabbled, almost incoherent with excitement. 'And now I am. Sort of . . . I don't suppose you'd consider giving me a cool nickname?'

Cutter just stared at him.

'I thought not,' said Connor, grinning. Then with uncharacteristic sensitivity, he abruptly realized that his tutor wanted to be alone – and left.

The anomaly shivered, enticing Cutter closer. He walked forward, staring fiercely into its glittering core as if sheer will could help him to see through to the other side. He touched its surface, watching the air ripple around his skin.

'Where are you, Helen?' he said softly, his voice too low for anyone else to hear. 'What do you want?' He glanced around him. Everyone was preoccupied. No one was taking any notice of him. He could just walk through the anomaly – and disappear.

But he couldn't move.

The past stood before him, enticing him with echoes of his lost wife. But behind him was the future – a world of uncertainty but also filled with hope.

Whichever way he chose to go, he was on the verge of something big.